Santa's Giving Heart

Written by Nancy Berke

Illustrated by Aubrey Hubbard

It is ever so quiet this early Christmas morn.

Joy fills our hearts
that Christ the baby
has been born.

Yes, Mary has a
newborn babe,
and Santa knows it too.

He wants to celebrate
this day.
He knows just what to
do.

Let all the children join in with candy, gifts, and toys.

It's a birthday party
for Jesus!
Let's share in all
their joys!

He gathers all his
elves around,
and shares with them
his dream.

Busy, busy all night
long,
their work makes Santa
beam.

And with that star shining bright above, Santa hastens to fill his sleigh.

He visits every single
child,
and upon their home
he prays.

Now Santa's through
with all his work,
this love Christ has
to share.

For each child,
he's filled their wishes,
to let them know he
cares.

And so my children,
we all give thanks
for the glory of
Christmas morn.

For Santa and his
giving heart,
when Jesus Christ
was born.

Santa's heart is meant
to share and God wants
us to know,
the love we give to
others is the way that
this will show.

CPSIA information can be obtained
at www.ICGtesting.com
Printed in the USA
BVHW091104061119
563072BV00003B/17/P